SIMMERING AWAY

Songs from the *Kanginshu*

Translated by
Yasuhiko Moriguchi and David Jenkins

Illustrations by
Michael Hofmann

WHITE PINE PRESS / BUFFALO, NEW YORK

Publication of this book was made possible, in part, with public funds
from the New York State Council on the Arts, a State Agency.

Printed and bound in the United States of America.

First Edition

Companions for the Journey, Volume 11

10-digt ISBN: 1-893996-49-2
13-digit ISBN: 978-893996-49-6

Library of Congress Control Number: 2005934744

Published by
White Pine Press
P.O. Box 236
Buffalo, New York 14201
www.whitepine.org

for David Jenkins and Jikihara Gyokusei

歌や歌へ
泡沫の
あはれ昔り
恋しさを
七十九翁書
偕楽

"Here seated quietly
at my desk
I have set down these songs
one by one
just as I recollect them
as my little memorials."

In sight of Mt. Fuji,
Autumn, 1518

First,
    a gentle opening
    of the flower-
    flecked brocade sash
    of her underclothing

then,
    all too soon
    a troubled heart
    like the willow-
    fronds twisting in
    the wind

now,
    will I ever
    lose this memory
    of her tousled hair
        in bed?

Whose love
has stirred
this fragrant
plum blossom?

oh spring,
from where
comes this arousal?

moon, speak
and come
to me

just for now,
plum blossom,
lie there,
singing softly,
under moon beams

Let go your hold
for I must hurry now
to fetch the water
for the tea,
but you ask me,
shall I come again?
oh, how tempting,
your novice heart

young leaves of tea
that newly sprout
        we pinch and
        we are pinched too,
are drawn,
and stirred to and fro
        for such is
        the very bloom
        of youth

        you are a vessel
        full of fresh
        young leaves of tea
        and once I dip within
        I forget
        all other, older tea

        yes I forget
        all other, older tea

We are apart
we are apart

> love ends in an empty dream
> just your memory shares my bed
> only loneliness surrounds me

> my tears flow
> in soundless waves
> streaming on my sleeves

will our rivers
ever meet again?

> will our rivers
> ever meet again?

Her eyebrows glowed
like living willows

now spring
will have ended
where she is
and my heart tumbles
    always
    with the weeping willow
    on the wind

with this wind
I will come
to your willow and
I'll sweep away
the dust from its shade
    I'll sweep away
    the dust from its shade

(away)
 simmering away
 our world passes
 simmers
(away)

Shimmering
     like the heat-haze
     his earthly form
     has vanished
away

     now ivy covers
     even the shape
     of his grave-
     stone

        'oh, set me free
        from this suffering!'

        and as he said it
        he was gone

        and as
        he said it
        he was gone

Let us sing,
    and sing of the love we have
    for the days that are gone,
    time like so much foam upon the water,
let us play
and have our fun now
and just
    as we free women
    plying in these boats
    live out our lives so
sing this one song

In my mind,
    turning
in my mind,
    turning

this tiny wheel
    our world
so quickly
whirls away

Wait for me
in the shade
of the willow!

and if anyone should ask
just say that you are
cutting off a sliver
    for a toothpick!

I love you
then I look on you
and love you
    all the more
and go
to lock the gate
within the hedge
    with lightened heart

The moon sets,
    our boat is moored
    the town is near
    for we can hear the temple bell

we lie,
    our pillows side by side
        rudder left
        rudder right
    we reach
    for each other,
wet with evening dew

Here comes
another boat
　　into the bay
there
the sound
　　creaking
　　clicking
　　oars dipping
　　in the shallows

The wind blows
and in my heart,
pain
            to think
            of the gale beating
            at the petals
            of the cherry blossom
            and of the time
            that flies so fast
            those rare nights we meet,
this rare night we met

Morning sounds of
    cloth being beaten
    reach me
        pat pat
the grief of parting,
        pat pat
    reaching back
    the sound of
tears upon my pillow

How frail
the knot that binds—

a half-bow
in a sash
of sky blue

My tears
        rain falling
        all night long
upon
        the plantain leaves
my pillow
        by my window

The moon has set
beyond the western tower

our time together
did not even last as long
as the cherry flowers

  so weak,
our bond was so weak
and my heart burns
    like the dying flame
    in the lamp

how hateful
to see myself like this!

what is there to do?
　　so what
　　is there to do?
this world is but a leaf
blown by the wind
upon the waves

　　　　all,
　　　　all of this
　　　　is a dream
　　　　　　phantasm,
　　　　　　foam upon the water
　　　　soon gone
　　　　in the time
　　　　the dew may vanish
　　　　from the bamboo leaf,
　　　　　　this irksome world

a dream!
illusion!
    dear God!

      but hard it is
      to look upon
      a joyless man

        this world is
            a dream within
            a dream within
        a dream

      (there he is)
      his face
      so damned sober

what good is it
  (I ask)
to be so sane?
our life time
is just a dream

        why not
just get crazy?

The windbreath
of love comes
　　entangling my sleeves

how heavy my sleeves!

such a heavy heart too
brings the wind-
breath of love

The love I feel
is like the firefly
    flickering
    by the water-side,
      silent
      sorrowful
      firefly

There is no time
I do not have you
in my heart

there is no night
when gently drowsing
I forget

In this world
    year by year
people age and die
while the flowers by my house
are in full bloom,
their colors and their fragrance
just the same as always,
    the flowers by my house
    are in full bloom
just the same as always

while I wonder
who will now take pleasure
in the sight of them
yet another year goes round
like a tiny wheel

with bitterness
I linger
in this world of sorrow
    like the waning moon

Who is this
        (you naughty boy!)
that hugs me tight
and bites me,
a married woman?

            but it's fun
            we're in full bloom
                    at seventeen
                    we're in full bloom
                    at seventeen

but nibble gently—
if your teeth leave marks,
then he will know

My hair
that I had just tied up
has loosened,
    gently tumbling,
    as my heart
    has fallen for you

How I envy
this my heart
        always with you
        night and day

the ecstasies of heaven
and the wish
to be reborn
as Buddha
all are hollow dreams

with love in your eyes
pour your wine
into my cup
pour your wine
with love in your eyes

The plum blossoms
are manhandled
by the rain,
the puffs of willow seed
by the wind,
　　　and always,
　　　our world
　　　by lies

The cock crows
      the moon stands
      above the thatched roof
      of the tea house
and on the frost-laden bridge
footprints
made him think it
time to leave

      already footprints
          on the frost-laden bridge

      but if I were now
      to cross that bridge
      then all would know
          my footprints;

      so let the tide ebb
      and I can cross
      at the river-mouth

beneath the bridge
the tiny fish
dart to and fro
   they too
   not wanting
   to sleep alone

You seem now to be
a thousand miles away
so let me
once again
    drink
    a little wine
    by myself
bring some comfort
to my own heart

The scent of fine incense
leaks through the reed screen

    cold wind in the trees

on such an evening
you can even sense
the fragrance of the moon

花籠に
月を入れて
漏らさじこれを
曇らさじと
守るか

大愚

Now this
is the all
and the ever—

    enter
        as the moon-
        beam slides into
        a flower basket

    hold,
        do not spill

    and unclouded
        keep its light

The songs in this book are from the *Kanginshu,* an anthology of poetry that appeared in Japan in the early 16th century. They were translated by Kyoto residents Yasuhiko Moriguchi and David Jenkins over a five-year period. As the translation was being completed, another Kyoto resident, Michael Hofmann, did a series of paintings inspired by the poetry. Michael's teacher, the great Nanga artist Jikihara Gyokusei inscribed the poems on Michael's paintings. These efforts culminated in an exhibition and a series of performances held in Kyoto in 1993. An original hand-made edition of *Simmering Away* was part of that exhibition. For the current edition, a few more songs and paintings have been added.

The poetry has been published in a fuller selection as *The Song in the Dream of the Hermit,* published by Broken Moon Press in 1993. The following is an excerpt of the original introduction written by the late David Jenkins, which may serve as a short introduction to the present volume.

"We do not know for sure the name of the man who assembled the songs in the *Kanginshu*. Other than what we can deduce from the themes and general tone of the poetry, we know almost nothing of the life or circumstances of the anthologist. Yet this man, clearly himself a poet of the highest order, inhabits every corner of this book, an impassioned, commanding intelligence.

"The shape of the collection is based upon that of the Chinese classic *Book of Songs;* that is, it comprises 311 songs. *Kanginshu* is firstly the product of solitary rememberings. Reflecting the collector's own cultivation, it is a repository of songs from numerous sources, from temple and theater, contemporary forms of poetry, as well as the minstral tradition. The songs are generally classified as *kouta*, or 'short songs.' But the collection also includes sixty longer songs from various *Noh* sources, and numbers of songs in other styles. It includes all songs that come from the quiet center, whatever their length, songs that convey truth—be they songs of the human voice, or those of the babbling streams, the falling leaf, the roaring dragon, or the five thousand books of the Daizo sutra.

"What seems to give this collection some of its power and vitality is the tension between acceptance of the transience of life and a barely concealed anger at its passing, along with a determination to focus smiling on the here and now."

COMPANIONS FOR THE JOURNEY SERIES
*Inspirational work by well-known writers in a small-book format
designed to be carried along on your journey through life.*

Volume 11
Simmering Away: Songs from the Kanginshu
Translated by Yasuhiko Moriguchi and David Jenkins
Illustrations by Michael Hofmann
I-893996-49-2   70 pages $14.00-

Volume 10
Because of the Rain: Korean Zen Poems
Translated by Won-Chung Kim and Christopher Merrill
I-893996-44-I   96 pages $14.00

Volume 9
Pilgrim of the Clouds
Poems and Essays from Ming Dynasty China
Translated by Jonathan Chaves
I-893996-39-5   192 pages $15.00

Volume 8
The Unswept Path: Contemporary American Haiku
Edited by John Brandi and Dennis Maloney
I-893996-38-7   220 pages $15.00

Volume 7
Lotus Moon: The Poetry of Rengetsu
Translated by John Stevens
Afterword by Bonnie Myotai Treace
I-893996-36-0   5 x 7   132 pages $14.00